TONI AND THE FABULOUS
BALLOON CHASE

Charles was sitting on the bed, leaning against the headboard. He gestured to the foot of the bed.

"Well," I said, plopping down and settling in for a long chat. "Your famly seems nice." Kind of a dull opener, but I wanted to start out easy.

"Yes. My mother's an angel. And my sister is great." He smiled. "When she's not being a stubborn eight-year-old."

"You really hate your uncle, don't you?" I blurted. So much for subtlety. It never was my strong suit, anyhow.

"I do," Charles said. "He killed my father."

"What?" I hadn't bargained for that!

Charles shrugged and faked a smile. "Never mind. I shouldn't be talking about this."

"Not fair," I said firmly. "I hate it when people start things and then won't finish them." I started to get up from the bed.

"Wait," Charles said, leaning forward and putting out a hand to stop me. "You're going to think I'm nuts, but here goes . . ."

Look for these other exciting
Adventurers, Inc. titles!

Ready, Set, GO!
Susette's Awesome Adventure
Rosina Saves the Day
Allison and the Big Apple

Adventurers, Inc.

#5:
Toni and the Fabulous Balloon Chase

Mallory Tarcher

Z*FAVE
KENSINGTON PUBLISHING CORP.

Z*FAVE BOOKS are published by

Kensington Publishing Corp.
850 Third Avenue
New York, NY 10022

First Printing: December, 1994

Printed in the United States of America

*This book is dedicated to
my oldest and dearest friend,
Gordon*

You can't turn back the clock. But you can wind it up again.

—Bonnie Prudden

Dear Mom,

I had a pretty good time in New York—kinda strange, not what I expected, but pretty good. Still, I'm glad to be heading to jolly old England, where I *don't* know anybody!

I miss you and the boys, but the four of us—Rosina, Toni, Susette and I—are becoming our own little family. It's nice having sisters after all these years of being the only girl!

Speaking of being the only girl, tell the boys I bought them each an "I Love New York" T-shirt, and if I can keep the rest of the Adventurers from using them as nightshirts, I'll bring them home with me when I come.

Love you lots,
Allison

Dear Mother and Father,

New York was wonderful. The city is so exciting. We saw a Broadway musical and the New York Public Library, and went horseback riding in Central Park.

If it weren't for the fact that I would miss all of you so much, I'd want to go to college there.

I'm looking forward to England. Rosina keeps saying how fabulous it is—she's been *everywhere*—and I can't wait to go to the Tower of London and see the Crown Jewels.

Give Grandpa and the twins a hug for me.

Love,
Susette

Dear Mama and Papa,

New York is still the most glamorous city in the world!

It wasn't quite the same traveling with the Adventurers as it is traveling with *you guys*, but the food was wonderful, the shopping unbeatable, and the city as exciting as ever!

I definitely want to go to college either

at NYU or Barnard! (That is, of course, if I don't get into the Sorbonne in Paris!)

I can't wait to get to England! I got us bumped up to first class. This trip is turning out not to be so bad.

John made me leave one of my suitcases in New York, so I have to spend the rest of the summer living out of only one bag. Oh well, I figure I'll shop along the way.

> Till we are together again,
> Love you,
> Rosina

Dear Mom,

I'm writing this to you from the bathroom of the first-class lounge of the 747 heading to LONDON! I know that sounds like a kind of weird place to be writing from, but I'm stuck in here and I don't have anything else to do. Wait, I don't mean it *that* way, it's just that once you've played with all the lotions and potions they have in here, and have washed your hands twice and pounded on the door for help lots more times than that, all that's left is writing home. HELP!!!

See, this really isn't my fault. It's Rosina's. She's the one that convinced the guy at the ticket counter to bump us all up to first class, so it's *her* fault I'm in *this* bathroom, not the one in coach. And I bet that the one in coach doesn't have a door that sticks!

We were late getting started this morning (we were having too much fun last night to get to bed on time), so I didn't get to put on my makeup or do my hair before we left for the airport. No big deal, I thought—I can get ready on the plane. So I took my bag into the bathroom, fussed around for a bit, did, um, you know, usual bathroom stuff, but when I tried to leave, the door was jammed.

The stewardess yelled through the door that they're trying to take the door off the hinge and rescue me, but I gotta say, Mom, this is the single most embarrassing thing that has ever happened to me. I mean, *ever!* And can you believe it, Debbie had the nerve to shout at me through the door that *I* was embarrassing *her!* Like I did this on purpose. I swear, Mom, she's even *more* bossy since she graduated from high school than she ever was—if you can believe it.

Anyhow, Mom, they're shouting something at me again, so I gotta go. Worse comes to worst, I can slip this letter under the door and somebody can mail it to you.

Love you,
Toni

One

"So there I was," I said to my best friend Allison Morris when they finally got me out of that bathroom. "Stuck! It was awful."

Allison giggled. "I think it's pretty funny! Typical you."

"At least it was a first-class bathroom. It would have been awful being stuck in coach!" Rosina Iglesias said, leaning over the arm of her seat and across the aisle that separated her seat from mine.

"Typical *you!*" I shot back.

"Hey! It's not my fault!" she protested.

"Right!" I snorted. "Oh, please," I said in a high voice meant to mimic hers, "please, Mr. Check-in Guy, couldn't we be bumped to first class?"

"Well!" Rosina was indignant. "Excuse *me* for getting us better seats!" And she turned away from me in a huff.

Nobody said anything for a minute. "I'm

sorry," I mumbled. I knew I was being a jerk, but I didn't think it was funny that I had spent the first hour of our flight in a toilet! I looked around. First class was nice. I shouldn't have been such a cow to Rosina.

"The seats are great!" I said by way of apology as I wriggled around on the sheepskin pad on the leather seat. "And lots of leg room!" I added, swinging my feet out in front of me.

"You sound like an advertisement!" Allison teased. "Try our first class," she joked. "Really short people can stretch out to full length."

I stuck out my tongue at her. Allison is tall, and she teases me all the time about being, well, "under tall." I hate the word short. I prefer to be called Vertically Challenged.

Luckily, before anyone could say anything else, the stewardess started our lunch service. Now, I don't know if you've ever flown first class (I hadn't before this trip), but *wow*, do they make a big deal over meals. It was six courses, with three different set of plates and silverware, and it took them at least two hours to get to the good part . . . dessert!

We had a choice of three main courses, Chicken Something, Beef Something, or Fish Something. Yeah. Right. Just what I wanted, fish served at 30,000 feet. *Not!* We all had the Chicken Something. But before that there were these little crackers with mushy stuff on them, pieces of melon wrapped in a type of ham (it's call prosciutto), and hot bread. *Then* a salad, *then* the main course. I was stuffed by the time we got to the salad!

Also, the stewards and stewardesses kept pouring different wines into our chaperone John McGonigle's glass (actually, they used three different glasses), so he was acting pretty goofy by the time dessert was served.

"This is the life!" he said, stretching his long legs out in front of him. "I could really get used to this."

"I know what you mean," my sister Debbie agreed. Of course, she had arranged it so that they were sitting together. Debbie has a *major* crush on John, which she's had since he was her teacher in high school. "It's so civilized."

Allison rolled her eyes. "Oh, yes, I *do* so prefer it," she said, sticking her nose in the air.

"Honestly!" I muttered.

"I think it's great!" Susette Yoshi was the only one who hadn't laughed hysterically when I finally emerged from the bathroom, so now I smiled at her instead of making some wisecrack. I figured I owed her one.

"Maybe with all those different wines, John'll fall asleep and we can share his cake or whatever it is," Allison whispered to me.

"This is first class, darling," I joked. "We can have our cake and eat his, too!"

Allison thought that was pretty funny, but there's something about flying first class that just stops people—even us—from being too rowdy, so we just sat back and relaxed while they brought out the dessert tray.

"Major yum!" Allison said under her breath.

The cart had every kind of dessert imaginable: cakes, pies, cookies, and other stuff that I couldn't begin to name.

Well, we all pigged out, and then spent

the next two hours of the flight trying to burn off all that sugar! Not an easy thing to do in a relatively small space.

Finally, John kicked the back of my seat. I turned around to see what was going on, and he was looming above my headrest. I didn't say anything. He leaned down and put his face right up close to mine.

"If you do not stop talking, wiggling, moving around. . . . In fact," he continued, "if you do anything other than sleep, I'm going to put you on the first plane back to California. Are we clear?"

At first I thought he was joking around, but the funny thing was, he had a really serious expression on his face. I nodded "yes," turned back around, and tried to sleep.

Sleeping on a plane always gives me these really bizzarro dreams. This one was sort of a montage, a collection of images, of the last few weeks. I saw myself getting the letter from the Santa Barbara Women's Council telling me I'd won the essay contest and was going to be traveling around the world this summer. Then I was watching the night the four of us "Adventurers" had first met.

Allison and I have been best friends, well, forever, but none of the rest of us really knew each other. We liked each other well enough from the start, but because we're all from pretty different backgrounds, it's taken us a while to get *really* close.

Rosina is beautiful, with long light brown hair and a gold American Express card. Her mother is French, her father Spanish. She's very sophisticated, but not as sophisticated as she'd like everyone to think she is. Which makes her fun to hang out with!

Susette is Japanese American. Her family is pretty strict, so this trip is a *real* adventure for her. I think she probably misses home more than the rest of us do. I *know* she misses her grandfather a lot! She writes to him almost every day.

Allison is tall, and black, with hair like Janet Jackson. She has five brothers, so this trip is cool with her. She gets *tired* of being the only girl! (Well, there is her mom . . .)

And I'm, well, small. I have long, curly brown hair which is constantly out of control. Kind of goes with my mouth!

Anyhow, in this dream, all of our adventures kept getting mixed up until finally, at the end of the dream, I was stuck in the first-class bathroom with a horse from the Claremont Stables in New York City. I guess my New York adventure and my most recent disaster got mixed up in my mind. Oh well. I was trying to get the horse to move out of the way so that I could get the bathroom door open, when the stewardess woke me up and started serving coffee.

Finally, we were descending over England!

Allison leaned over me to stare out the window.

"Can you see anything?" I asked. She was squishing me into the seat back so hard that it was all I could do to breath, let alone check out the view.

"No," she answered glumly. "Just clouds."

"Then get up." I pushed her back over the seat divider. "I'll let you know if there's something to look at!"

"England is always rainy," Rosina said. "At least it's always been rainy whenever I've been here."

Allison looked at me and shrugged. Rosina and her parents had traveled all over Europe. We knew we were going to have to put up with quite a bit of "know-it-all-itis" from Rosina for the rest of the trip.

"So, Rosina," I said, hoping to deflate her ego just a bit, "did you meet much royalty when you were here last? Have tea with the queen or anything?"

Debbie, who was sitting next to John in the row behind me, banged my seat. I popped my head up and glared at her. "I'm just asking a question!" I protested.

"Actually, we did," Rosina said with a smile. "A lord and lady. We met them at the races and had lunch with them at their house."

"A country house?" Susette asked. "I hear they're amazing."

"No." Rosina looked uncomfortable. "A small house in the heart of London, actually."

"Oh," I said in a knowing voice. "Impoverished royalty. How nice for you."

"Actually, lords and ladies are not royalty at all. Technically, they're the nobility, or as they say in England, the *peerage*. Some lords and ladies are born titled, because their families are part of the nobility. Others have been made lords and ladies by the queen for service to their country," John explained.

"Boy! Wouldn't that be great!" I was getting excited. "Let's do something really fabulous so that we get ladyized!" I suggested.

"The term is knighted, not ladyized," Debbie said, with a roll of her eyes. "And I'd prefer if you guys did *nothing* fabulous, and *nothing* scary, and just acted like normal teenage girls. Okay?"

I was about to say something smart back to her when I flashed on my dream and realized that in the short time we had been traveling, we had gotten lost in the mountains outside of Vancouver, thrown overboard while white-water rafting down the Colorado, stranded on an almost deserted island while sailing off the coast of Maine, and hooked up with a homeless boy we set out to help while taking a civilized horseback ride in Central Park. I guess Debbie had a right to a quiet trip to England. Just as I'd decided to give her a break, the wheels of the plane touched down at Heathrow Airport.

"Sure thing!" I offered, as I grabbed my bag from under the seat. "Whatever you say, Deb."

Allison looked over at me. I knew she couldn't figure out why I was agreeing so easily, so I winked at her and lifted my hand from behind my bag. She grinned. I had my fingers crossed.

Two

Heathrow Airport was *huge*. It was like a small city, with shops, restaurants, even a dry cleaners.

I nudged Susette and pointed it out to her. "A dry cleaners?" I asked.

"I guess it's for people who get dirty between flights." She shrugged. "I dunno, seems weird to me, too!"

John somehow managed to round us all up and herd us to customs. We were getting to be better travelers now. One carry-on each, and even Rosina had been whittled down to a single huge suitcase.

". . . and don't say anything stupid!" Debbie warned. No big deal. She was being her usual bossy self.

"I know, I know . . ." I said, thoroughly disgusted with the babyish way she was treating us. "Customs is no joke!" I had learned my lesson the hard way on our first trip through Canadian customs. I had jokingly told the guy behind the counter that John and Debbie were white slavers. I mean, it was a *joke*.

We stood in the customs line for what seemed like forever. "Hey, listen," Allison said. We all looked around.

"What?" Rosina asked.

"Listen to the way everyone is talking," Allison insisted.

"What about it?" Susette couldn't figure it out either.

"Listen to their *accents*," Allison said. "Isn't it exciting?"

"Well, we *are* in a foreign country," I pointed out. I still didn't get whatever it was she was trying to make us see.

"I know *that!*" Now she was getting irritated. "But doesn't it sound weird, their talking English, but *not*, really?"

When Allison got no response from any of us she shook her head and said, "Oh, never mind!"

I felt bad for her. I hate it when people don't really get what I'm saying, so I shut up and tried to pay attention to the voices around me. Maybe if I tried, I could find what it was Allison thought was so funny.

And then, I got it. Now that I was paying attention, it *was* strange. "They sound like they're in a movie, like *Oliver Twist,*" I said excitedly.

Allison smiled. "Exactly," she said. Rosina and Susette just shrugged.

Allison's observation made me realize something else, too. See, all airports look the same. For all I knew, the plane might have left New York and somewhere over the Atlantic, turned around and landed there again. The only thing that *really* stood out as different was the sound of people's voices. Suddenly, I really felt like I was somewhere *different,* somewhere exotic. It wasn't the place that mattered—it was the people in that place.

Finally, we made it through customs without a hitch. (In case you're wondering, I kept my mouth firmly shut the entire time and let John do the talking.)

"Thank goodness," John muttered as the customs official stamped our passports. "We're outta here! Come on!"

We pulled, dragged, and pushed our bags out of the customs area. "Are we being met by a car?" Rosina asked. "This suitcase is heavy!" she complained.

"Well, if you hadn't stuffed everything

that should have gone into the suitcase I made you leave behind into this one, it wouldn't be," John grumped. But Rosina's complaining had had the desired effect. John traded suitcases with her. "And, *no!* We aren't going to be met by a car. We're in London, ladies. We'll take the tube!"

"The tube?" I asked.

"That's a subway. They call it a tube because it goes through a tube in the ground," Debbie explained.

"Thank you Ms. Webster," I joked. You know, like in Webster's Dictionary?

"I've had enough of subways, thank you!" Allison groaned as John herded us over to a booth.

"Get in!" he said, pushing me toward the curtain.

"Why?" It was one of those photo booths you see at carnivals and malls. "I'm not riding all the way to London in *there!*"

"Don't be silly. You guys are getting student passes," he explained. "Good for one week of sightseeing in jolly old London. We take these photos over there," he said, pointing at a ticket booth, "and they give you a photo I.D."

Allison and I looked at each other. "Cool!" she said.

"Can we take a group picture first?" Susette asked.

John and Debbie sighed in unison. "I should have guessed," Debbie moaned. "Go ahead. But make it quick!"

We climbed into the booth. Allison and Rosina shared the hard, red, plastic seat and Susette and I sat on their laps.

"I'm getting wrinkled. Don't sit so hard!" Rosina protested as I plopped down on her lap.

I stuck out my tongue at her just as the camera snapped.

We had to wait two minutes until it developed. The machine spat out four identical one-inch snaps. "Lemmie see! Lemmie see!" We crowded around Allison, who had grabbed them as they came out of the machine.

"Oh great! All you can see of me is the side of my head and my tongue!" I moaned.

"I like it!" Susette was grinning. "It's your best side!"

"Enough, you budding models." John grabbed the pictures. "Come on! I don't want to spend the whole day in the airport. One at a time, now."

We took our individual pictures, then traded the extra three until we each had one of everyone else's, and headed over to get our student I.D.s.

The tube in London is nothing like a New York subway. The seats are padded fabric, not plastic, and there's no graffiti *anywhere*.

"I told you Europe was more civilized!" Rosina whispered. "Look, no litter!"

"And nobody is pushing!" Allison added as we took our seats, suitcases between our legs, on the Picadilly Line to London.

It was close to forty minutes later when John finally said, "Next stop, everybody off."

We emerged from the "Underground," which is another word that the Brits use for subway, into driving rain.

"Nice," I said as I struggled to get my umbrella open. "It's like looking at the world from inside a shower stall!"

"Get used to it!" Debbie said cheerfully as she pulled up the hood of her waterproof poncho. "We're in England, now!"

Luckily it was only a block or so to the

bed and breakfast. "Mrs. Beasley's," it was called.

Mrs. Beasley herself opened the door. " 'Ello," she said. "You must be the Yanks booked in for the week."

I didn't dare look at Allison. I knew we'd start giggling. She sounded just like a character on one of those funny English television shows that you can see on PBS.

"John McGonigle," he said, sticking out his hand.

"Pleasure, I'm sure." She nodded at the rest of us. "Come in, loves, you'll catch your death standing in the rain." She stepped back into the hallway to let us in. Mrs. Beasley was a plump lady in her early fifties, I think. (I'm not very good at guessing people's ages. Especially *adults'* ages. I mean, when you're fourteen, the only thing that really matters is that they're *older* than you are—and that gives them the right to tell you what to do!) Her orangish hair was done up in a bun, and her cheeks were round and rosy. Her dress had little flowers printed all over it, and she was wearing an apron and comfortable, if ugly, shoes. She seemed nice. Kind of like

a grandmother from a greeting card com-
mercial. A *British* one.

The house looked like it had once been
a real home, not a kind of hotel, with just
the bare minimum of changes made to
turn it into a place of business. John
signed us in at the small writing desk that
Mrs. Beasley used for her office, and then
she handed us our keys.

"I've put the young ladies on a different
floor than you two." She looked at John
and Debbie. "That all right?"

"Preferable!" Debbie said, a bit too
loudly, I thought.

Luckily for Rosina, who was acting like
her suitcase had gained weight since she
packed it, we were only on the second
floor. Actually, we *were* the second floor.
There were three bedrooms and one bathroom . . . and the bathroom was down
the hall.

Allison and I bunked together in the
large room, while Rosina and Susette each
took a small one.

"See you guys in half an hour in the
lobby. Okay?" John said as he paused on
the second-floor landing before carrying
his and Debbie's bags up one more flight

of stairs. (He'd abandoned Rosina to her suitcase fate at the check-in desk.)

"Cool!" Allison called out as she unlocked the door to our room. "See you then!"

"Wow." Not terribly descriptive, but all I could think of to say as I shoved my suitcase in the door. The room was so, well, so English! The two beds were narrow, but covered in white embroidered comforters. Matching horse prints hung above the wrought-iron headboards, and braided rugs covered the polished wood floor. A small fireplace with a gas log was located against the far wall, and two windows let in the grayish light from the street.

I looked at the narrow dresser and single closet. "Boy, I hope Rosina's room has a bigger closet than this," I said as I hung up my clothes, "or she'll be . . ."

There was a knock at the door.

"Who is it?" Allison called out.

"Rosina! Can I borrow some closet space?"

". . . in here using ours," I finished under my breath. "Sure!" I shouted. Rosina's outfits were really fantastic, and her

clothes fit me better than the other girls'
did, so I was being a little selfish by agreeing.

By the time she had finished hanging
up her stuff, Susette had joined us and
was sitting on my bed.

"Do you think we should check up on
them later?" Rosina asked, nodding her
head toward the third floor where John
and Debbie had their rooms.

"*I* think they need a chaperone!" Allison
agreed. "How about you, Toni? After all,
Debbie is your sister!"

"*No!*" I practically shouted. "Remember
what happened last time we meddled!" It
had happened when we were at the Grand
Canyon. See, we'd thought that Debbie and
John were perfect for each other, and we
were afraid that if something—or someone—came between them, our trip would
be over, so we told a bunch of, well, I
guess "lies" is the only word for it, to the
two other people they were sort of see-
ing . . . and things got a little out of
hand. Actually, we barely made it out of
Arizona alive, and it wasn't only the river
that almost got us. It was Debbie.

"Come on, let's go sightsee." Rosina

popped her head out of the closet where she was still rearranging our clothes. "I can't wait to see all those jewels in the Tower . . ."

". . . I can't wait to try fish and chips," Allison said, rubbing her stomach. "I'm starving."

"I can't wait to ride on the top of a double-decker bus!" Susette grinned.

"And *I* can't wait to go to the bathroom." I paused at the door to the hallway. "I haven't peed since we left American airspace. Meet you downstairs."

I walked a total of about two feet when I turned back and called, "If I'm not there in five minutes, someone bring a crowbar."

Three

It was still raining when I joined the rest of the gang in the lobby. Debbie was looking irritated (her hair always frizzed up in the rain), Rosina looked bored (that's her usual expression unless we're shopping), Allison and Susette were staring out the window, and John kept looking impatiently at his watch.

"One kid," he said as I tromped down the stairs. "One is definitely enough!"

"Gee," I said as sweetly as I could, "Debbie always told me she wanted four, didn't you Deb?"

The four of us girls dissolved into giggles watching Debbie turn purple and John a bright shade of pink!

It never really poured, but neither did the rain ever really stop. We walked for what seemed like miles.

"Everything here is so old," I commented as we passed old building after old building, some of which had been built before the United States was even born.

We started our official walking tour at Buckingham Palace. I thought the building itself was kind of boring looking—kind of like a library—but the Royal Guards were outrageous!

There were a whole bunch of these guys dressed in red jackets, black pants, and these giant black fur hats—kind of like big, black Q-Tips on their heads!

"Excuse me," I said to the one nearest the gate. He ignored me completely.

"Excuse me!" I said a bit louder. I hate it when people act like I'm not there. "Is the queen at home?"

"They're not going to answer," Rosina said, grinning.

"Why not? Don't they like tourists?" I asked.

"They're not allowed to talk to anyone. Not for any reason," she answered knowingly.

"Boy." I shook my head. "That's sure not a job *I* could do!"

We got bored standing around in the

drizzle, so we wandered over to the Royal Mews. That's where the queen keeps the horses that pull her carriages.

The horses lived in style. Their stalls looked like they'd been licked clean (yech) and were decorated with brass ornaments everywhere. Still, there was no way to get away from the fact that underneath all the decoration, it was still just a barn.

I took a deep breath. "Smell that?" I asked Susette. "What does it remind you of?"

She sniffed. "The stable in New York?" she answered.

"Yep." I took another deep breath. "No getting away from it!"

"I guess barns smell the same the world over." She shrugged. "Let's get out of here!"

Rosina squawked because she wanted to stick around in case the queen came out, but the rest of us were starving. We set out after John who promised to take us someplace good for lunch. He must have been on some sort of secret fitness kick because I swear he had us walk for miles! When I complained—loudly—he responded with, "Just a few more blocks."

"I'm starting to feel more like a fish than a person. We've been underwater since we landed," Allison moaned.

"What are *you* complaining about? I have to take five steps to every one of yours," I muttered, my thighs sore from trying to keep up with her longer strides.

Rosina said, "You're even looking a little bit like a fish. You know how their eyes sort of pop out . . ."

"Enough! Any more talk about fish and I won't be able to eat one for lunch." Debbie jogged ahead to catch up with John, our inexhaustible leader.

Finally, after swimming our way through half of London, we had lunch at a little fish-and-chips place in Piccadilly Circus.

Piccadilly Circus used to be the "red light" district, *not* a good neighborhood, but now it's mostly filled with tourist shops and video arcades.

I had barely finished licking my fingers clean from a wonderfully greasy lunch when John started prodding us to "get a move on."

Now, I was starting to get tired. It felt like post-lunch nap time to me, and when I'm tired, I get cranky.

"No more walking." I refused to budge

from the restaurant's wooden bench. "My feet hurt, my belly is full. Can't we just hang out for a while?"

We compromised. John threw us onto a double-decker bus.

"Race you to the top," Allison said as she leapt up the small circular staircase. Rosina and Susette took off after her.

"Wait up!" I shouted as I elbowed by Debbie. "I hate having short legs!" I muttered.

The rain didn't bother me as much now that we were riding as it had while we were hoofing it. I guess walking with an umbrella is an art that you just don't learn living in sunny Santa Barbara, California.

Debbie and John stayed below, so we four goofed around until the bus conductor poked his head up onto the deck.

"Baker Street, young ladies," he said, tipping his cap. "Everybody off."

"Boy, he sure is nicer than the New York bus drivers," Susette whispered as we exited onto the street.

"Why here, John?" Rosina asked, looking around.

"I know!" I shouted. "Sherlock Holmes lived here!"

"Sherlock Holmes was just a character

in a book," Susette said, laughing. "He didn't *live* anywhere."

"Oh yeah," I argued. I had spotted a bronze plaque on a nearby wall. "See, the Sherlock Holmes Museum."

The museum had more Sherlock Holmes stuff than I could have imagined. For example, there was his pipe, his violin, and a mock-up of his study.

"Oh . . . what case is this from?" I asked, pointing to a quill pen. "Wait a minute, lemme think . . ."

"How do you know about all this stuff?" Rosina asked.

"She's always wanted to *be* Sherlock Holmes," Allison answered.

"Indubitably, my dear Watson!" I agreed. "I think being a detective would be sooooo cool. Sneaking around in the dead of night . . ." I said, making my voice all spooky.

"Right!" Debbie snorted. "You're afraid of the dark."

She had a point there. Still, she didn't have to blow my fantasy like that.

"I'd be a good detective. I know I would," I said grumpily. I hate it when Debbie is right about anything.

"Well, Madam Detective, if I don't get to see those crown jewels soon, I am *not* going to be a happy person at all!" Rosina said, nearly stamping her feet.

"Ohhhhh," I said, drawing back in mock fear. "Come on, John, or she'll have us thrown in the Tower of London and beheaded."

"I can't take any more sightseeing today," Susette said. "I vote we do the Tower another day, and take one of those nice big black cabs back to Mrs. Beasley's."

"Noooo!" Rosina howled. "I want to see the jewels! You guys promised!"

But she was outvoted, so home we went. That's the funny thing about being on the road. Wherever you spend the night is home, even if you've never been there before.

Four

The next morning we saw something I never thought I'd see in England . . . the sun.

John had rented a minivan so that we could spend a leisurely day in the English countryside. Big mistake!

First, it was like a game of Chinese fire drill. You know that one? It's where everybody gets into the car, then, without opening any doors you climb around inside trying to get into another seat. It's funnier to do than it sounds . . . and it was all John's fault anyway, for getting in the wrong front seat. He forgot that the driver's side in England is different from the driver's side in America. Somehow, *I* ended up on the driver's side. Well, *that* wasn't going to work, and by the time we all got settled, I ended up way in the back, Debbie ended up in the front passenger's seat, where John had been, and John ended up where I had started. In the driver's seat.

John started the car. I guess that when you've been driving on the right side of the road for your entire adult life, switching to the left is hard. At least that was the excuse he gave us for nearly hitting two pedestrians and then getting stuck on the roundabout (what they call traffic circles in England) for a full fifteen minutes. By the time we got to the actual "countryside," we were terrified, and John was white lipped and even whiter knuckled.

Still, the countryside, believe it or not, was worth *Mr. Toad's Wild Ride*.

As London fell behind us and we left the suburban houses (which looked like suburban houses everywhere), rolling green hills and dense woods took over the view. The farther from the city, the less the little towns looked like tacky imitations of what an English town should look like, and the more natural and real they became. Like neon gave way to fake rustic signs that, in turn, gave way to *real* rustic signs. Cars parked by the side of the road, which had dominated the landscape near the city as they do near any city, were now outnumbered by horses and cattle grazing on the other side of stone fences. Even John, who was *not* having a good day, was smiling by the time we left the last sign that said YE OLDE WHATEVER in our rear window.

The road we were on was mostly two lanes in each direction, but every time we came to a town, it became like a regular street, with two-way traffic and a lower speed limit. And there were roundabouts everywhere—it seemed like we ran into one every five miles.

"When are we getting on the freeway?" I asked John. "I mean, if we're driving all this way, shouldn't we take a superhighway?"

"This *is* the freeway," John said. "Or the closest thing to it, anyway. The roads in England are just smaller than American ones."

"So are the lorries," Rosina added.

"The what?" Susette asked.

"The lorries—that's what English people call trucks," Rosina explained. "They don't have humongous eighteen-wheelers like we do. English lorries aren't much bigger than delivery vans."

How weird, I thought.

"And there's actually a car called a Mini," said John.

We all cracked up over that—imagine trying to sell a car called a Mini in America!

"Bold, sleek, stylish, sexy—the 1995 Mini," I said in a TV announcer's voice. "Zero to sixty in . . . oh, about three minutes."

We went through little towns called Farnborough, Fleet, Basingstoke, and Andover. The farther we got from London, the cuter the towns became. The farmland in between was really pretty—small fields of incredibly green grass, set off by low stone fences and tall hedgerows of purplish-green bushes.

Occasionally we passed by a farmhouse with a real thatched roof—meaning the roof was made out of bundles of *straw,* all strapped together and piled two or three feet high. The straw hung over the windows and doors like neatly clipped bangs.

"That house looks like it needs a bit of a haircut," said Allison.

We were all agreeing on how adorable the little thatched houses were—until I opened my big mouth.

"Yeah, but think of all the bugs that could

live in that straw—eech," I said. "Not to mention the *rats*—right over your bed at night, their little feet scritching through the straw . . ." I made scritching sounds with my fingernails on the seat cushion.

"Eew, cut it out," said Rosina. "I'm sure there aren't any rats, and they're very cozy inside."

"Maybe," I said. "But I'm glad the roof of *my* house isn't made of edible material. . . ."

The beautiful green land we were driving through was pretty flat, though sometimes it rolled in gentle hills.

"What's this area called, John?" Debbie asked.

"Salisbury Plain," he said.

"Salisbury . . ." Rosina repeated. "That sounds familiar—"

"Don't tell us," Allison said.

"I've been here with my parents," we all chanted.

"No, I *haven't*, as a matter of fact," Rosina said. "But isn't Salisbury Plain where—"

Rosina's jaw dropped.

"What?" we said. All of us (except John, of course, who had his eyes on the road) were staring at her.

"Stonehenge!" Rosina whispered, and pointed to the front of the van.

We whirled around—and there it was. Stonehenge, the famous circle of huge gray stones, was in a broad green field just off the road we were traveling.

"Cool!" we all shouted at once.

John pulled into a parking area on the far side of the road from the monument. Then we walked through a small pedestrian tunnel (called, weirdly enough, a subway) back underneath the road to get to the Stonehenge side.

You've probably seen pictures of Stonehenge in magazines or on TV. But until you see it in real life, you can't appreciate how . . . *eerie* it is.

"It's *so* ancient looking," Susette murmured.

"Yeah," said Allison. "I can just picture a bunch of old druids dancing around it in the moonlight."

John held up his guidebook, "Actually, it says here, that Stonehenge was erected by Bronze Age tribes about four thousand years ago—two thousand years before there were druids in Britain."

"Wow," I said. Some of the tall, narrow

stones had other stones laid crossways on top of them, like doorways for giants. "I wonder how those ancient people managed to get those big rocks up on top of each other?"

"No one really knows," John said. "The book says the stones came from a quarry in Wales, almost a hundred miles away. How did the people manage to move them here without machines?"

"Maybe a sorcerer, like Merlin, did it," said Susette.

"Or maybe it was *aliens*," I suggested.

We all stood in silence and just gawked at the huge stones for a few minutes, then slowly walked around the whole circle. I swear, I could just *feel* the vibrations coming from it—Stonehenge is a really magical place.

Finally we crossed back under the road and piled into the van.

"Anyone getting hungry?" John asked when we were out on the road again.

"Yes!" the Adventurers shouted together.

"They say English food is pretty awful," said Debbie. "Boiled beef, cabbage, kidney pie—"

"That's disgusting," said Allison.

"—blood pudding," Debbie finished.

"Oh, please!" I said. "There is no *way* I'm eating something called blood pudding!"

"Don't worry," John said reassuringly. "Salisbury town is just a few miles from here, and I was thinking we'd stop"—he put on a fakey English accent—"for a spot of tea."

"Great!" said Rosina.

We stared at her like she was nuts. "I don't think *tea* is going to fill me up," I said. "I'm *hungry.*"

"English tea isn't just *tea,*" she explained. "It's tea, plus scones with clotted cream and marmalade and butter, and crumpets, and cakes, and biscuits, which is what English people call cookies, and—"

"Okay, okay," I said. "We get the idea."

Just then we came over a small rise, and in the shallow valley below us was the prettiest little town I'd ever seen. The houses and shops were mostly red-brick, two or three stories high, with reddish-gray tile roofs. The streets were narrow and ran at crazy angles to each other. We crossed over a small river with willows hanging over it, and ducks and geese walking up and down the bank.

John parked the van, and we got out to walk to the tea shop. Even in the center of town, it seemed like every house had its own little garden in back, where the people grew strawberries and tomatoes and lettuce.

Linden's Tea Shop was like heaven. I'm still not too big on tea (I prefer hot chocolate, actually), but I am stark raving *mad* about scones and clotted cream. (For those of you who, like me before the Linden's experience, don't know what scones and clotted cream are: Scones are like large, buttery, fluffy biscuits, but better than any biscuit in the world; and clotted cream is like a cross between sweet butter and whipped cream, only yummier than either one. Put a dollop of clotted cream on your scone, pop it into your by now heavily salivating mouth, and you're having the Linden's experience. Definitely worth every one of its 10,000 calories.)

An hour later, we staggered out of Linden's Tea Shop, stuffed to our hairlines with scones, strawberries, cakes, and tea.

John was studying his city map of Salisbury carefully.

"Should be just around that corner," he muttered to himself, and started down the sidewalk. When he got to the corner, he stopped, turned, and grinned. "Ladies," he said, "welcome to Salisbury Cathedral."

I guess it sounds kind of weird getting all excited about a church—but this was no ordinary church. Salisbury Cathedral was a gigantic gray-stone building in the Gothic style (that means, basically, that it has lots of narrow, pointy, arched windows everywhere), with an incredibly tall steeple at the center. It stood in the center of a wide, green, perfectly trimmed lawn, which somehow made it seem even bigger and taller and grayer and more impressive.

John told us that lots of people consider Salisbury Cathedral the most beautiful church in England, if not the whole world. He also told us that a famous English painter named Constable spent practically his whole career just painting the cathedral from different angles, in different weather, and at different times of day.

At first I thought Constable probably needed to get a life. But after looking at the cathedral for a while, and noticing how it stood out against the sky and the pretty little town in the background, I began to understand why a painter would love it so much.

We did a quick tour of the inside, which was almost as impressive as the outside. (The coolest thing inside the cathedral was the burial slabs that made up parts of the stone floor. Seems that if you were rich enough, you could pay to be buried *inside* the cathedral, where tourists would walk on your grave for the rest of eternity. What an honor!)

At last we trooped back to the van, where all of us (except our chauffeur John, of course) took naps as Salisbury faded into the distance behind us.

When we woke up, the first thing out of Rosina's mouth was, "Are we there yet?"

"Just around this bend," John answered cheerfully. "I hope," I heard him mutter under his breath. Like most men, John has a thing about asking directions. As in, he won't. Oh, well.

We were going to Maldleigh House, which for generations has been the coun-

try seat (as they say in England) of the
Hastings family. In the old days, Lord and
Lady Hastings would have given great
hunting parties and balls and stuff for
their rich friends. Nowadays, lots of the
old families don't have as much money,
and they have to open their houses to
tourists who, for five pounds (or about
eight dollars in American money), can
walk around and see how the nobility used
to live.

And let me tell you, they lived pretty
darn well.

Maldleigh House was shaped like a gigantic, three-stories high *H*. The entrance
was in the "crossbar" of the *H*. To the left
was the west wing, and to the right the
east wing.

You walked up a broad flight of steps
to get to the double front doors, which
were—no joke—at least twenty feet high and
eight feet across. On either side of the
doors were three stone columns, which
went from the ground to the top of the
third floor. There were bigger-than-lifesize
statues on the edge of the flat roof, all
the way around. I read the names carved

into the stone underneath the statues: Aristotle, Pliny, Shakespeare, Newton . . .

"How many rooms do you think it has?" I whispered to Allison.

"Who knows?" she said, shaking her head. "Sixty, seventy, maybe."

"I've never seen anything like this in my life," Susette murmured.

John and Debbie were equally awed by the humongousness of the house.

Only Rosina seemed underwhelmed. She was nodding her head appreciatively. "I think maybe I could get used to living here," she said coolly. "If I absolutely had to."

"Rosina!" we all shouted.

"Okay, okay," she said, laughing. "I admit, it's nice."

"Nice!" we shouted.

Suddenly, over the shoulder of one of the statues, I saw a spot of color in the sky.

"Look!" I pointed.

"What?" Rosina said. "Is it the queen?"

"Prince Charles?" Susette guessed.

"Who? Where? I don't see anyone in any of the windows," said Allison, peering intently.

"Not in the windows!" I said. "In the sky, behind the house. And it wasn't the queen, *or* Prince Charles. It was . . . I'm not sure what it was."

By the time they'd figured out where to look, it had sunk behind the roofline and out of sight.

I turned to Rosina and the others. "Honestly, what *is* it with you guys?" I said. "You're all so into royalty. I don't get it. They're just like us!"

"Only richer," John joked.

"You just wait," Rosina snorted. "If you're lucky enough to meet anyone with a title, I bet you end up all tongue-tied."

"I've known her for fourteen years," Debbie said. "I wouldn't count on it. Now, Toni," she said to me, "you're not having visions of sky divers again, are you? No more jumping out of airplanes! At least not as long as I'm on this trip with you."

"Yeah, okay," I said. "And not till I'm eighteen." (I had made a tandem skydive in Vancouver at the start of our trip, and I guess I'd gotten kind of boring on the subject.)

We queued (pronounced "cued") up, which is what the English say for "got in line," for a tour. The woman who was leading the tour looked like your basic Sunday-school teacher: tweed suit; flat, really ugly shoes; saggy stockings; hair in a bun, and buck teeth. In fact, she looked sort of like a horse. She told us her name was Mrs. Hardley.

"This is going to be a real laugh riot," I muttered to Allison.

"Yeah, right up there with a visit to the dentist," she whispered.

"Ladies, is there something you'd like to share with the group?"

You guessed it—she was talking to us. And the tour hadn't even started yet!

We walked through the huge center hall of Maldleigh House, and through the windows at the back of the hall, I saw what I'd tried to show my friends: There on the great lawn out back were two big, beautiful hot-air balloons.

"Ooh, John," I said quietly, tugging at his wrist. "Can we—"

He turned and saw the balloons, and his face went an unusual shade of grayish red—kind of like the roofs of the houses back in Salisbury. *"No!"* he muttered.

Mrs. Hardley paused in her lecture

about the tapestries hanging in the hall and gave John a dirty look.

John smiled at her meekly, then whispered to me, "No riding in balloons, no jumping *out* of balloons, no balloon anything!"

"Party pooper." I scowled, then went back to paying attention to the tour—which turned out to be pretty interesting.

The Adventurers took bets on whether Mrs. Hardley's stockings would fall down and, if they did, whether she would trip on them.

"Can you imagine the parties they used to give in here?" Rosina said, clearly awed.

"Can you imagine the heating bill," I muttered, shivering. "England is *cold*. It's summer, and I haven't been warm since we landed!"

Mrs. Hardley marched us on to see the old kitchen with a huge wood-burning fireplace where the food was cooked, and a pump from which the servants drew water.

We wandered through bedroom after bedroom, and sitting room after sitting room. All the rooms had been furnished at various times throughout the nineteenth century.

"This stuff doesn't look very comfortable," I said, pointing at a spindly wooden chair in the fourth bedroom. "That chair doesn't look like it would hold even *my* weight."

Mrs. Hardley and the rest of the group had already moved into the adjoining sitting room.

"I dare you," Allison said with an evil gleam in her eye.

Well, I'm not one to back down from a dare, so I plopped down on the velvet seat. The chair gave a loud creak. I have *never* moved so fast in my life! I was out of that chair, across the room, through the door, and at Debbie's side before Allison even knew what was happening.

She dashed into the room with the rest of us and slammed to a stop right next to me. We tried not looking at each other, but it didn't help. We spent the rest of the tour giggling! I mean, I know it was wrong, and I wouldn't make a *habit* out of sitting on museumlike stuff I'm not supposed to sit on, but . . . Well, you know what I mean.

The one *really* cool part of the tour was the Ancestors Hall. Paintings of dead people lined the walls from one end to the other. The first few paintings were kind of goofy-looking—not so much from the costumes the people were wearing (though those frilly collars, not to mention the *tights* the men wore, were a trip), but because the artist couldn't paint! I mean, the people looked incredibly stiff and awkward—they had these expressions on their faces like they were being pinched really hard but weren't allowed to show it.

Farther down the hall the costumes were less weird, and the painters got better, too. Then at the end of the hall, the people were in modern-looking suits and dresses—which was strange in its own way. Somehow it's weird to see a person dressed like your neighbor (at least, your neighbor on a formal occasion) in a big elaborate oil painting.

I noticed that most of the people in the paintings were called the Duke of This, the Earl of That, or the Viscount of Whatever. And most of them had the last name Hastings. Talk about fancy-schmancy.

By the time the tour was wrapping up, my feet were sore, my mind was numb, and my bladder was bursting! We had been walking for *hours*. At least for a long time.

"Do you think the people who lived here ever got lost?" I whispered to Allison.

"Probably," she whispered back. "I couldn't find the front door now if I tried!"

I shrugged. "I don't even care where the front door is. I need a bathroom!"

"I think I saw a ladies' room over through there," she suggested, pointing back through the Ancestors Hall.

"Okay. Thanks. I'll catch up with you guys in a bit." I backed out of the group, then edged my way along the wall until I found the entrance to the Great Hall. Once safely out of eyeshot of the formidable Mrs. Hardley, I breathed a huge sigh of relief.

"There has *got* to be a bathroom somewhere!" I muttered. "Even in the old days people had to pee." I started marching down the hallway. The huge portraits of the generations of Hastingses seemed to be watching me.

Like those pictures in a fun house, I thought. My pace quickened. *What a creepy looking family! I wouldn't be surprised if there's*

*a few skeletons in their closets—like, maybe a
murderer or two!*

I couldn't find a bathroom anywhere. I
had opened three doors already, but no
luck. One was a broom closet; another led
into the drawing room where a group of
British schoolchildren were starting their
tour; and the third led to a hallway that I
hadn't seen before. Since I could eliminate
the broom closet and the drawing room as
possibilities, I decided to follow the hallway
and see where it led. Unfortunately, it
didn't seem to lead to a bathroom! I was
starting to get really worried. At the end
of the hallway, I stopped and looked both
ways. To my left was a balcony, so I
headed right, down the next hallway. Still
no door with a picture of a girl on it.
(Although at that point I would have used
the men's room with no problem!) I followed this hallway around a bend to the
bottom of a staircase.

The staircase was blocked at the bottom
by a red velvet rope, the kind of rope that
marks the lines outside of movie theaters
and nightclubs. By now, I was almost dancing in place. "This isn't funny!" I said
aloud. "I'm *not* enjoying this at all!" My

bladder made my decision for me. "I'm going up!" I announced to no one in particular, as I hopped over the rope and took the stairs two at a time.

The main part of the house had been immaculate. I could tell no one had really lived in it for years. But the part of the house I was entering now had a sort of shabby, lived-in look. Suddenly, I heard a noise. It sounded like fighting, not the kind where brothers and sisters are yelling at each other and calling each other names like chucklehead and chicken-butt, but the kind where people are blowing things—and each other—up. I ran toward the noise, which I figured had to be coming from a television or something like that, and ended up in front of a closed door. It was either go in and hope whoever was there knew where the bathroom was, or wet my pants. I opted to go in.

I opened the door to the first normal room I'd seen all day. No pictures of dead people wearing funny wigs. No chairs that looked like they'd break the minute you sat down. No rugs that had probably been nice once, but now were so old and thin that all they were good for was wall art.

Just a normal bed, with regular sheets, a regular desk with a halogen lamp, and a boy playing what I guessed was "Mortal Kombat" on his Nintendo system. He was sitting in a big chair, his back to me. All I could see was his head.

"Excuse me . . ." I said.

No response. He must have been too absorbed in his game to hear me.

"Excuse me . . ." I tried again, only louder this time.

Still nothing.

"Hey you!" The time for subtlety was over. I was desperate.

He jumped up in surprise. He looked familiar somehow. And all he was wearing was his underwear.

"What are you doing in my bedroom?" he shouted, moving back behind the chair.

"Looking for a bathroom. What are *you* doing in your underwear?" I asked.

"It's *my* bedroom. I can wear what I want," he said in a really cute accent.

I was beginning to feel pretty stupid. "Look, if I can use your bathroom I'll get out of your hair. I'm sorry, but I really need to go."

I guess he took pity on me because without saying a word, he pointed to a door on the side wall.

"Thank you," I said with as much dignity as I could muster while running almost knock-kneed across the room. I have never, ever, been so glad to be somewhere.

By the time I had finished and emerged from the bathroom, the boy had put on a pair of pants. Both of us, I think, were much relieved! Now I felt okay about actually *looking* at him. He was about fifteen or just sixteen, with blond hair that fell over his very blue eyes. Cute, I decided, very cute!

"Uh, thanks," I began. "I'm Toni." I offered him my hand.

He ignored it.

"I washed!" I said indignantly.

I guess he realized he was being rude. "I'm Lord Hastings," he said, still without offering me his hand.

"Right," I said. "And I'm Princess Di."

He looked shocked, then angry, and then he started to laugh.

"What's so funny?" I demanded.

"You are," he said, grinning. "Princess Di is much taller than you are."

"And I'm sure Lord Hastings is much

more *polite* than you are!" I *hate* height— or, lack-of-height—references.

He stopped grinning. "I'm sorry," he said, finally extending his hand. "That was very rude of me. I'm Charles."

"Prince Charles, I suppose." I was still mad.

"No," he said, starting to smile again. "Charles Hastings. I really *am* Lord Hastings."

"Oh." Now *I* was the one who felt stupid. I realized why he seemed familiar. He looked like the people in the paintings hanging in the Ancestors Hall. "Should I call you 'your highness?'" I asked.

"Charles will be fine."

There was an awkward pause.

"Thank you for letting me use your bathroom. I was desperate," I said, starting to blush. This was not a normal conversation to have with a guy! Especially a *cute* guy.

"No problem."

"How can you be a lord when you're so young?" I asked bluntly.

"My father died," he said, looking angry again. "So the title is mine."

"Oh." I seemed to be saying that a lot.

"I'm sorry. Mine's dead, too. But I'm not a lord." *He's going to think I'm a complete idiot*, I thought.

"I'm sorry," he said. And it sounded like he meant it. "For your father, and for snapping at you."

I shrugged. "He died when I was pretty young. I can barely remember him." For some reason, I suddenly felt that "crying lump" in my chest. It had been a long time since I had cried about my father.

"What are you doing here?" he asked. "Not here, here . . ." he said, gesturing around the room. "In England, here. On holiday with your mother?"

"No." I grinned. "I'm here with the Adventurers." I told him all about how we four were chosen winners of the essay contest, and about some of our adventures so far this summer.

". . . and Rosina will never, ever believe I've been standing here talking to you. She's got royalty on the brain!" I grinned at him.

"Boy," he said wistfully, "it sure sounds like you guys are having fun. There aren't many adventures to get into around here.

Besides, it's no fun having adventures when you're alone."

I had an idea. "Well, why don't you come with us?" I offered.

"Pardon?" Charles asked.

"Come back to London with us! We're going to see a musical in the West End tonight. I'm sure we could get another ticket for you!"

"No." He shook his head. "Thank you, but I can't."

"Oh." There was that word again.

"I'd love to, really, but I have to stay with my mother and little sister." His face darkened. "They need me."

I thought I knew what he meant. When my dad died, my mother and sister and I stuck together like we had been Super-Glued at the hips. I shrugged. "Okay. Well, I'd better get back to the group. I'm sure they've sent out an alarm by now." I turned to leave. I was disappointed. Having Charles join us had sounded like fun.

"Say . . ." He put a hand on my shoulder to stop me from going. "How about if you and your traveling companions come back tomorrow night and spend the weekend? I can show you around the estate, and we can go hot-air ballooning. . . . I'm sure my mum won't mind."

"Your mom won't mind your inviting *six* people for the weekend? *My* mom would kill me!"

"It's not like we don't have the bedrooms." He grinned. "Should I have my mum ask your guardians?"

"You'll have to! I can just imagine the look on John's and Debbie's faces if I waltz down the stairs and say that Lord Hastings has invited us to his country house for the weekend." I told him where we were staying in London. "Can you show me the way back down to the entry hall? I don't want to spend the rest of my trip lost in your house!"

After putting on a shirt, Charles led me right to where the "private" rooms met the "public" ones. "See you tomorrow!" he said as he jogged back up the stairs. "I'll have my mum call. Mrs. Beasley's on High Street Kensington, right?"

I gave him a thumbs-up, and headed off to find my friends.

Five

We were all piled into one of those huge black London cabs, heading home from the theater. We had seen the Sondheim musical *A Weekend in the Country. Very appropriate,* I thought.

"I *did too* meet Lord Hastings," I cried.

"Right." Rosina still thought I was lying. We had been arguing since I'd rejoined the group that afternoon.

"I don't care if you met the queen and her corgies, I don't want to hear another word about it!" Debbie was starting to look major-league stressed out.

"Do you think spending the weekend at Charles's house will be anything like the show we saw tonight?" I asked Allison, purposely ignoring both Rosina and Debbie.

"Sure," Allison said loyally. "I just hope nobody gets shot and no one hangs himself."

"I guess," I said doubtfully, glaring at

Rosina. "Although it might be kind of interesting . . ."

"If we actually get an invitation, I'll eat my raincoat," Rosina snorted.

"Stop it!" Susette looked like she was going to cry. "You two are making me crazy!"

I stopped. Susette never yelled. I guess if you are normally a calm person and then you get uncalm, it has more of an impact than if you are noisy all the time. Food for thought, but I had a feeling that calm isn't something I was ever going to be able to fake.

Please let there be a message from Lady Hastings, please, I silently prayed. And, amazingly enough, my prayers were answered!

"Here," I said, handing Rosina my raincoat while John read us Lady Hastings's note. "Eat mine. Yours is more expensive!"

Rosina plopped down onto one of the overstuffed chintz couches in the entry hall to our boardinghouse. "I can't believe it. I'm actually going to a country house for a weekend soiree."

"A what?" I asked.

"She means a party," Allison clarified.

"Whoa, slow down." John, as usual, was

fighting to stay in control. "No one's going anywhere so fast."

Needless to say, we all started talking at once. Even Debbie joined in on our side. "Come on, John," she said, taking his arm, "you know we always try to really see what it's like to *live* somewhere, not just to do the tourist thing. Besides, with an entire country estate for the girls to run around on, we might actually get some time alone."

John turned slightly pink for about the millionth time this summer.

"Yeah!" I jumped in. "You won't see us for the whole weekend. We promise—right, girls?"

We all nodded our heads so hard, we looked like those silly, wobbly-necked dogs you see in tacky souvenir shops and in the back windows of some old people's cars.

"Oh, *no!*" Rosina suddenly screamed from her place on the chintz couch.

"What?" we all answered in unison.

"I don't have a thing to wear." She looked like she was going to burst into tears.

"You have the world's largest suitcase," I said disbelievingly.

"But all my *good* clothes are in the one John made me leave in New York," she accused.

"Your *worst* clothes are better than our best," Allison protested.

Rosina, wisely, said nothing.

"Of course, we could always say no to the invitation," Susette teased.

"That's okay," Rosina said quickly. "I'll make due." She sighed dramatically.

We each looked at John and held our breath.

"So, I take it this means you all want to accept?" he joked. "Then I'll call Lady Hastings in the morning, and do just that!"

I don't think John had ever been hugged so hard by so many people at the same time. "All of you, *get* up to bed," he said with mock severity, and frightened of his changing his mind, we *got!*

The next morning, Rosina was even more determined to buy something new to wear at Maldleigh House.

"Levi's are fine!" I insisted as we dressed the next morning. "We're *teenagers*,

Rosina. Just bring that baby-doll dress you got in New York for dinner."

"Levi's? Levi's? Are you out of your curly head?" Rosina was standing on my bed, shouting.

"Look." I put my hands on my hips. "I am wearing jeans, a nice top, and my loafers. Do what you want." She finally settled on velvet bellbottoms, a white ruffled shirt, and lace-up boots. A little strange in my book for eight o'clock in the morning, but that was Rosina, all over.

We were due at the Hastings' that night in time for dinner. That left the entire morning free for shopping. And, with Rosina leading the charge (no pun intended), we hit every store in London.

Debbie had a great idea—for once—and we dragged Rosina away from the stores on High Street Kensington (which only *she* could afford) and into the street market on Portabello Road.

A lot of the kids there looked really strange. It seemed that punk was still alive and well in England. There were more people with nose rings than you would believe!

I took out one of my globe earrings

(each of the Adventurers had a set). "What do you think?" I asked, holding it up to my nostril.

"Ewwwww!" Susette started to giggle. "I don't care what the rest of you do, I am *not* putting a hole in my nose!"

"No piercing of *any* body parts!" John joked. "I want to give you back to your parents just the way I got you!"

We kept walking, past a coffee shop and a store that sold used guitars, until Allison stopped at a stall selling a bunch of tourist stuff. "You guys slept in the "I Love New York" T-shirts I got my brothers, so maybe I'll get them these," Allison teased, holding up a pair of jockey shorts made with the design of the British flag.

"Not!" we shouted back.

For the rest of the day we shopped, giggled and pigged out on fish and chips. Rosina kept whining about wanting to go to Harrod's for tea.

"Hey, Rosina," I mumbled, my mouth full of half-chewed chips.

"What?" She turned around to look.

I stuck out my food-coated tongue.

"Never mind," she said, nose in the air.

"Harrod's is *definitely* not the place for you."

I grinned at Susette. I was beginning to get the idea of how to handle Rosina!

By the time we loaded ourselves into the mini van and headed out to Maldleigh House, we were as stuffed as a Christmas turkey and had just about the same amount of energy. I slept most of the way there, and, when we finally pulled into the driveway, I felt halfway human again. Of course, I did have to go to the bathroom. *Oh well,* I reasoned, *at least this time I'll know where it is.*

Rosina was still muttering about her wardrobe, as she insisted on calling it, as we pulled up the long driveway to the estate.

"There they are!" Allison leaned over me to point out the window.

"Stop squishing me!" The biggest problem with being eighty pounds is that people think nothing of shoving you out of the way.

From his upstairs bedroom winndow, Charles must have seen us start up the long driveway, because now the whole family was waiting out front to meet us. Charles, who was even cuter than I remembered him, was standing with his mother, a beautiful blond woman who was, by the way, wearing jeans. A little girl of about eight or nine, who I assumed was Charles's sister, held on to Lady Hastings's hand, and behind them stood an older man who looked a little like Charles.

We piled out of the minivan in our usual disorderly manner, and then, suddenly shy, stood in a line waiting to be introduced.

Since I was the only one who had met Charles, I stepped forward. "Hello, Lady Hastings, I'm Toni. Thank you for inviting us." A little formal, I thought, but my mother would have been proud.

"This is John, Debbie, Allison, Susette, and Rosina," I continued.

Everyone else said "Hi." Rosina, true to form, curtsied.

Lady Hastings smiled at me. "I just knew you were Toni. You're just as pretty as Charlie said you were."

I lost the next few things she was saying

as I tried to wrap my brain around the fact that Charles had said I was pretty.

". . . this is Sarah," Lady Hastings said, pushing her daughter forward, and Charlie and Sarah's uncle, Randolph Hastings."

"A pleasure to meet you, Lord and Lady Hastings," Rosina piped up when she realized that for once, my mouth was failing me.

"*I* am Lord Hastings," Charles corrected. "Uncle Randolph is my father's *younger* brother."

"Quite right, Charlie." Uncle Randolph spoke for the first time. "Shall we help these young ladies with their luggage?"

Charlie scowled. "Right," he said, grabbing the nearest two bags. "Follow me."

I grabbed my own bag and trotted along side of him. *He sure is touchy about that lord stuff,* I thought. "This is really cool," I said, struggling to keep up with his longer strides. "We're going to have a great weekend. I can tell." I always babble a bit when I'm nervous.

Charles kind of grunted at me and continued toward the house.

* * *

Charlie and Lady Hastings, who asked us to call her Lucy, showed us to our two adjoining rooms. (Debbie and John were being put up in rooms in another wing.) And boy oh boy . . . were they amazing!

They were huge, with high ceilings, and two beds each, beds that had probably been around for hundreds of years. (I think the sheets had been changed more recently!) As usual, Allison and I roomed together.

"Why don't you girls get into something comfortable," Lucy said, looking pointedly at Rosina's boots, "and then we'll have dinner."

By the time we got ourselves cleaned up and downstairs, Lady Hastings, Charles, Sarah, John, and Debbie were already in the dining room.

Charles showed us to our seats, and took his place at the head of the table.

"Wouldn't you like your uncle to sit there, dear?" Lucy asked.

"No." Charles scowled at his mother. "*I* am the head of the family. It's my place."

"Charles." His mother's voice carried a warning tone.

"He is *not* my father," Charles said through clenched teeth.

Sarah looked like she was about to cry, and our heads were going back and forth between them so fast, I was getting dizzy.

"It's all right, my dear." Uncle Randolph had entered the dining room without anyone noticing. I found myself blushing on his behalf. "Dinner will be equally delicious no matter where we sit. Right, ladies?" He smiled at us, trying to make light of what was an embarrassing moment. "Lady Hastings is an excellent cook."

I was a little surprised that Lady Hastings had done the cooking herself, and then I remembered what John had said about old families that still had the title and the land, but none of the money that used to go with it.

Anyway, the food was simple but great, and I had a good time passing peas between my plate and Sarah's. *She* started it . . .

Most of the dinner conversation centered around royalty.

"Have you met Princess Diana?" Rosina asked.

"Just once," Lucy said. "At the wedding."

"Noooo . . ." Rosina looked like she was going to faint.

"Oh my god!" Allison sputtered. "I saw a videotape of that!"

"What was it like?" I asked. "Tell us, please."

"She looked so pretty," Susette added.

We were all babbling at once.

"Well," Lucy said, leaning forward as she began to tell her story. "No matter what has happened to the royal couple since, it was a truly beautiful wedding. It was the most exciting social event of the century."

We listened, mouths open, our food growing cold as Lucy spun her tale. Rosina listened so hard she put her elbow in her dessert! "Wow. That's just the kind of wedding *I* want."

"Not me," I said. "Too many thank-you notes! I want something small and simple . . ."

"Nothing is simple around you!" John interrupted. "Except this—it is *simply* time for all of you girls to go to bed. Sarah has already fallen asleep at the table."

He was right. She had. But at least she

hadn't put her elbow in her pie, like Rosina!

Before we could protest, Lady Hastings spoke up. "Good idea," she said. "The balloons fly first thing in the morning. If you girls are planning on being dressed and ready to go by seven A.M., you'd best get to bed."

Well, as used to arguing with John as we were, not even I was going to argue with a real live "lady," even if we were on a first-name basis.

"Randolph, will you carry Sarah upstairs for me . . ." Lucy began.

"I have her." Charles had swept Sarah into his arms before Uncle Randolph could even push back his chair. "I'll put her to bed, Mother."

"I'll help!" I offered. I figured it would give me time to talk to Charles alone. Something was going on with him and his uncle, something bad, and I was curious. Uncle Randolph seemed okay to me, but Charles had spent most of the evening looking like he wanted to deck the older man!

Lady Hastings sighed, then blew Charles

a kiss. "Thank you, dear," she said. "Sleep tight, all."

"I just don't know what's gotten into him . . ." I heard Lady Hastings say as we left the dining room.

I glanced at Charles, since he was clearly the "him." Charles had heard her as well. I saw his jaw tighten and his eyes narrow.

The Adventurers trooped up the stairs, Charles struggling only a bit under Sarah's weight.

The other girls offered to help us put Sarah to bed, but I shot Allison a look, and taking their cue from her, the Adventurers suddenly got "very tired" and headed off to their rooms like they were running from a fire.

I grinned. Sometimes, I just *love* those three. I knew they thought they were giving Charles and me some time alone, but at that point, I was more curious about why Charles hated his uncle than I was about kissing him or something. (Well, actually, I was equally curious about both!)

We got Sarah to bed without too much trouble. I mean, Sarah wasn't a baby or anything. And clearly, Charles had been taking care of his sister for a while, now.

I wasn't sure what to say as we turned out the light in Sarah's room and closed the door behind us. I didn't want to go to bed yet. I wanted to spend some time with Charles, but I wasn't sure what to say. I figured I'd start with an old standby. "Can I use your bathroom?" I asked.

Charles looked at me and raised one eyebrow. I loved it when he did that.

"Sure," he answered. "You know the way," he added as he led me to his bedroom.

I futzed around in the bathroom long enough to make it look good. When I came out, I noticed that the only light in the room was coming from Charles's desk lamp. Charles was sitting on the bed, leaning against the headboard. He gestured to the foot of his bed.

"Well," I said plopping down, crossing my legs underneath me, and settling in for a long chat. "Your family seems nice." Kind of a dull opener, but I wanted to start out easy.

"Yes. My mother's an angel. And my sister is great." He smiled. "When she's not being a stubborn eight-year-old, that is."

"You really hate your uncle, don't you?"

I blurted. So much for subtlety. It never was my strong suit, anyhow.

"I do," Charles said. "He killed my father."

"*What?*" I hadn't bargained for that!

Charles shrugged and faked a smile. "Never mind. I shouldn't be talking about this."

"Not fair," I said firmly. "I hate it when people start things and then won't finish them." I started to get up from the bed.

"Wait," Charles said, leaning forward and putting out a hand to stop me. "You're going to think I'm nuts, but here goes." I settled back down and he took a deep breath. "My father was Randolph's older brother. Even when my father was alive, Randolph was always hanging around here. I think he had a thing for my mother from the start. Then, one day he and my father were supposed to go hot-air ballooning . . . Well, at the last minute Randolph *didn't* go, and there was an accident, and my father died. *You* figure it out."

I was silent for a minute. I didn't know what to say. I mean, Charles's story didn't exactly prove anything, either way. "I know you miss your father," I said slowly. "But do you really think Randolph *killed* him? Are you sure you're not . . ."

"Yes." Charles stood up and walked over to the window. He put his hands in his pockets and stared out at the stars. "I *am* sure. And I'm also sure that my mother is falling for Randolph."

I thought about it for a moment. She *had* looked at Randolph with kind of goofy eyes. But that didn't necessarily mean she was in *love* with him, did it? "Maybe she's just lonely," I suggested. "My mom dates sometimes." I looked down at my knees. "I hate it, too. No one will ever replace my father. I don't care how wonderful the guy is. But that doesn't mean she shouldn't date." I walked over to join Charles at the window.

"My mum won't hear a word against him, either," he said, his voice tight. "I think he's stealing from the estate, old artwork, silver pieces. But when I tried to tell her my suspicions, she slapped me." Charles's expression was angry. "I'm not a child. I am the man of this family. I can help her, but she won't let me." His face softened then, and he added, more gently, "My mum's having a really tough time."

I reached over and put my hand on his shoulder. I wanted to say that it would be all right, but I really didn't believe it. Things sounded awful. And sometimes things *didn't* come out right, no matter how hard you wished they would.

"I hate that we have to have the house open to the public," Charles went on. "We never did when my dad was alive." His voice grew low and scratchy. "Everything's gone wrong since then."

I felt my eyes start to sting. "I know. That's how I felt for the longest time after my father died. And I was so young, too. Much younger than you . . ." I looked at Charles and could see that he was fighting tears. "Look," I said in my brightest voice, "we're going ballooning tomorrow. That'll be fun, won't it?"

He nodded.

I knew he wouldn't want me to see him cry, so I started to leave. And then, I stopped, ran back over to him, and, standing on my tiptoes, gave him a kiss on the cheek.

" 'Night . . ." he said softly as I turned away.

I almost went back to him, but I heard him sniff, so I just kept walking and closed the door behind me.

Six

Allison was still up when I got back to our room.

"Hey." I flopped, fully dressed, onto my bed and stared up at the ceiling.

The connecting door to Rosina and Susette's room opened before I got to say anything else. They came running in and joined Allison on her bed.

"What happened?" Susette asked.

"Did you guys kiss?" Allison asked. "I mean, *really* kiss?"

"You kissed a real lord?" Rosina looked like she was turning green around the edges.

"What?" I hadn't really been listening to my friends' chatter.

"Earth to Toni," Allison said, and the others looked at me like I was nuts.

"He hates his uncle," I said, which wasn't really an answer to any of their questions, but it was what was on *my* mind at that moment.

"Duh," Rosina said. "We have eyes, you know."

"What's up, Toni?" Allison was the only one who had switched gears quickly enough to realize I was going somewhere with this statement.

Still on my back, I crossed one leg over my other leg and started to swing my foot. That's my best thinking position. "Charles thinks his father was killed by his uncle Randolph, who says it was an accident, but who is now dating Charles's mother and, according to Charles, stealing things."

There was a moment of silence as everyone sorted out my pretty dramatic sentence.

"Wow," was the general consensus.

"Uh, Toni," Rosina began, "are we about to get into trouble?"

"Excuse me?" I said, eyebrows high. I was offended by her implication. Me, a troublemaker? "No, we are *not* going to get into trouble. How could we? All I said was . . ."

"We got the idea," Allison said. "I think Rosina just wants to know if *you're* going to do something that we're all going to get scolded for."

I sat up. "No," I said sadly. "There's

really nothing I *can* do. I'm not even sure Charles is right about his uncle."

I looked carefully at my three friends. "And yes," I added, "I *did* kiss him." It was none of their business that it was just on the cheek.

They grinned at me. They'd got what they wanted. "Now, go to bed. I can't wait till morning. Ballooning sounds great," I said, starting to get undressed.

Susette and Rosina got up to leave. "What do you wear to a balloon?" Rosina asked.

Allison and I both threw our pillows at her.

The next morning dawned bright and clear, very un-English, but I took it as a good sign. Rosina, sensible for once, decided to let us set the fashion trend and showed up in Levi's and a sweatshirt. The sweatshirt had CHANEL written in big letters across the front, but at least the outfit was semi-normal.

By the time we got down to the front lawn, John and Uncle Randolph had inflated the hot air balloons. Charles was sort of hovering nearby, watching the men.

"What's John doing setting up a balloon?" I whispered to Allison.

"I don't know." She shrugged. "Maybe he has hidden talents."

The balloons were amazing to see, kind of like round circus tents, in every color you could think of, gently bobbing up and down, and held to earth only by their tie-down lines. At the bottom of each balloon was a giant wicker basket, like a picnic basket without a lid.

"All right ladies, here's the plan," Uncle Randolph began. "I am going to fly one balloon, and John will fly the other."

"What?" Rosina squealed. "Do you know *how?*"

John grinned. "I spent four summers during college taking people for balloon rides in the wine country. Piece of cake."

I must have looked doubtful. "Come on Toni . . . have some faith," he urged.

"*I* trust you, John," Debbie said, slipping her arm through his.

Allison and I looked at each other and made barfing noises.

"I'm going with Sarah," Charles said loudly. "Why don't you come with me, Toni, in this balloon, and John can take the others."

Now there was an idea I liked!

Just getting in the balloons was an adventure. Uncle Randolph got in first, and Charles handed Sarah up to him. I clambered over the rim of the basket. Then Charles went over to the other balloon to help the other girls get in.

John and Allison had already climbed in, but I guess Rosina wanted some help so Charles gave her a leg up. You know, a leg up is when the lifter stands with his hands linked in front of him and the 'liftee' uses the hands like a step. Well, Charles gave Rosina more of a boost than she had expected, and she went flying over the rim of the basket and right into Allison's arms! They ended up in a very undignified tangle of limbs at John's feet.

"Sorry," Charles said, trying not to laugh. (Sarah and I lost the battle.) He tossed the tie-down ropes into the basket.

Rosina was still too impressed with Charles's being noble to say anything, but she looked like she really wanted to bawl him out. Charles must have known, because he was *still* laughing when he got into our balloon. I was glad to see him having a good time. He'd been a little snippy when he'd insisted on riding in the same balloon as Sarah, but aside from that, he seemed to have gotten past the melancholy mood he'd been in when I'd left him last night. Still, I decided I'd keep my eyes open and see if Randolph acted suspiciously. Of course, I wasn't sure I'd know what that meant until I saw it. . . .

Suddenly there was a noise like a dragon's roar.

"Ahhhh!" I screamed and jumped into Charles's arms.

Sarah started laughing so hard, she had to hold her stomach. "You girls are funny!" she managed to say.

"What was that?" I asked when I found my voice, which had temporarily followed my heart into my tennis shoes.

Sarah pointed at the fire pot beneath the hole in the bottom of the balloon.

"That heats the air in the balloon and makes it rise," Randolph said, pulling down again on the lever, which triggered another burst of flame.

We were rising now, and I could see that John's balloon was doing the same. In between the bursts of noise, the ride was totally silent. In no time we were well above the trees, and the wind was gently blowing us over the estate. It was beautiful up there, but I could feel the temperature dropping.

"Is it colder, or is it me?" I asked.

Randolph checked the altimeter attached to the side of the basket. "Two of your Fahrenheit degrees per thousand feet up," he answered. "We're now at 4000 feet, so it's 8 degrees colder than on the ground. Charles tells me you have a little experience with altitude. A skydive, I believe."

"Don't get her started," Charles moaned. "Once she starts, she doesn't stop. It's her favorite subject!"

I hesitated for a moment. Had I really talked that much at breakfast? I must have. But that wasn't going to stop me from talking now!

"I did a tandem in Vancouver. It was great. It's kind of like this, actually. I mean, the part where you're under canopy is. The freefall part is pretty noisy, but . . ."

"Enough!" Randolph laughed and put his hands over his ears. "That sounds too dangerous for me. I'll take ballooning anytime."

Chicken, I thought. And then I wondered

how he could say that ballooning was any less dangerous than skydiving, when his own brother had been killed in a ballooning accident. And then I realized that Charles hadn't told me any of the details of his father's accident. I decided to listen and watch Randolph more closely.

Sarah had been standing by herself, but she came over to the other side of the basket to join us. "Tell me about America, Toni. Is it all like Disneyland?" she asked.

I had visions of Mickey Mouse running around the main street in Santa Barbara, with Goofy close on his heels and Minnie shopping her way through our town. "Not really," I said, "but where I live is nice." I grinned at her. "You should come visit sometime."

"I'd like to. Uncle Randolph said he'd take us all, but Charlie says he won't go. And Mummy says we can't go without Charlie." She looked accusingly at her big brother.

Her chin was looking a little wiggly, so I put my hand on her shoulder. "Maybe Charlie will change his mind," I said, but glancing over at Randolph, and then back to Charles's grim face, I really doubted it.

"Oh, look. There's the other balloon!" Sarah pointed at John's balloon, which had blown up alongside of us. "Hello, everyone," she called, leaning against the edge of the basket. "Oh, I hate being little," she added. And then she boosted herself up on the rim of the basket.

"Sarah!" Uncle Randolph shouted. "Come down from there at once!"

Sarah turned around to look at her uncle. "What?"

"Look out!" Charles screamed.

It happened in slow motion. As she turned, she lost her grip on the edge of the basket. Just as she started to go over the side, Randolph lunged past Charles and reached for her. She continued to fall.

It was horrible, just watching her go over the edge.

"Sarah!" I could hear John screaming from the other balloon.

Randolph was leaning against the edge of the basket, making it tilt wildly to that side. "Her foot's caught in the rope," he shouted.

I leaned over the edge, making the bottom tilt even worse. Sarah was dangling five feet below the balloon, her foot tangled in the tie-down rope that was attached to the bottom of the basket.

"Honey, are you okay?" Randolph yelled.

"Help! *Help!*" We could hear her call out.

"Out of my way," Charles cried, rushing to my side to look over the edge.

Randolph turned to me, his face white. "I can't pull her up by the rope from here. I can't reach it, and I'm afraid she'll come loose."

Charles looked like he was going to be sick. "It's all right Sarah, I'll save you," he called.

He sounded confident, but I knew he didn't have a clue about what to do next.

I looked over the edge again. I took a deep breath. "I can reach her," I said.

"What?" Randolph looked at me like he thought I was nuts.

"Lower me to her. Hold me by my ankles and I'll grab her. You can pull us both back in."

"No. I'll do it," Charles said.

I shook my head. "You're too heavy. It'll be easier to pull me."

"*Sarah. Sarah!*" I could hear John and

the others shouting to us, but couldn't make out much of what they were saying.

"Let's just do it," I said firmly.

"You're sure?" Randolph asked, his voice low.

"Help! Help!" Sarah's voice reached us again.

I nodded. "Just give me a second."

While Randolph tied a rope around my waist for safety, I thought back to what my tandem master Ranger Magee had taught me about fear. I closed my eyes. I pictured my fear. It was a hairy ball in my stomach. I took deep breaths and with each exhale tried to push the fear down deep. I knew if I could just get the fear around my hips, I could handle it. I mean, who cares if your butt is scared? I opened my eyes. "Ready," I said.

"Aren't you scared?" Charles whispered to me as Randolph grabbed me around the waist.

I felt the fear welling up inside of me again. "Thanks for reminding me," I muttered, and then I was face down, staring at the ground, 4000 feet away. I stopped looking at anything but Sarah.

"Hang on Sarah!" I shouted. Randolph

had me by my ankles now. I imagined Charles holding his uncle's waist and pulling back to help anchor him. My head was below the bottom of the basket. I stretched my hands down, but Sarah's ankle was still six inches away.

"I can't reach!" I shouted. "Further!"

Randolph lowered me another foot, and I got a good grip on Sarah's calf. "Got her!"

Sarah was crying. "Hey, it's okay, I have you," I called, trying to calm her down. "Stop wiggling, Sarah."

Inch by inch, Randolph pulled us up. I was barely clear and in the basket again before Randolph had reached down and gathered Sarah into his arms. Her arms flew around his neck and she started to sob.

Charles grabbed his sister out of Randolph's arms. I could see he was crying as well.

"It's okay, Sarah," I said, putting my arm around her. Then Randolph grabbed me in a hug.

I looked over Randolph's shoulder at the other balloon. "Excuse me, but I think

John is going to have a heart attack if we don't land."

Randolph let go of me and looked over. John *did* look more than a little red in the face, and he was pointing frantically toward the ground.

We landed our balloons, and Charles climbed out of the basket with Sarah in his arms. (I must say, she was kind of struggling to get down and stand on her own two feet. It struck me that Charles tended to treat her like a baby and not like an eight year old. He was definitely overprotective—probably because of everything that had happened.)

"How could you!" He glared at Randolph. "I never should have allowed Sarah in your balloon."

I looked at Randolph. His jaw had dropped. "Charlie . . ."

"*I'm* the one with the title. If you want it so badly, take me on, not Sarah. Killing her wouldn't help you, you . . . you . . ."

"Charlie, how could you? I would never . . ." Randolph faltered.

But Charles, Sarah in his arms, her head on his shoulder, had stormed off.

Randolph looked as if he was about to

cry. When he'd regained control of his emotions, he said, "I'm sorry you had to witness that. You see, Charlie thinks I killed his father." He shook his head, and then went on. "You were very brave, Toni, You saved Sarah's life."

I thought it was an abrupt subject change, but I guess Randolph didn't want to talk a lot about being believed a murderer. Not that I blame him.

John's balloon had landed a moment earlier, and now John joined Randolph and me. He grabbed my shoulders and turned me to face him. "How could you have . . . thank God you did . . . I was so frightened when I saw . . ." He was babbling.

Debbie reached us next and wrenched me out of John's grip. "Are you crazy!" she hollered, and then burst into tears.

The arrival of Allison, Rosina, and Susette saved me from Debbie's emotional outburst.

"Leave it to you to turn a peaceful morning's balloon ride into an adventure," Allison teased, but I could tell from the look on her face how scared she'd been.

Susette just hugged me.

"Weren't you scared?" Rosina asked.

"There is no courage without fear, Rosina," Randolph said quietly. "It's not bravery unless you are afraid. If you're not afraid, it's just stupidity."

Real courage is going to be telling Lucy about this, I realized. *After losing her husband, she won't take kindly to almost losing her baby,* I thought as we all walked back to the house. *Maybe she won't find out . . .*

As we approached the house, Lucy came running out to greet us. "I guess Charles told her," I muttered.

"Hanging out of a balloon," Lucy scolded as soon as we were in earshot. She looked like she didn't know whether to hit me or hug me.

Lucy made the right choice and gave me a huge hug. "Thank you," she said, and hugged me again. Then she grabbed Randolph. "I couldn't have borne losing her . . ." Lucy stopped, her voice choked with tears.

"Lucy, Charlie thinks . . ." he began.

"I know." She went white lipped. "I'm sorry. This has only made things worse."

I wasn't sure what she meant, but I felt sorry for her. For them all. Lucy and

Charles and Sarah were all such nice people—and I thought that maybe Randolph
was too. He certainly hadn't done anything
bad to me, and he was the first person
Sarah had turned to when I'd pulled her
back into the balloon. And to be honest,
I didn't remember Randolph being anywhere near Sarah when she went over the
basket's rim. Hadn't he yelled at her to
come away from the edge?

I sighed. *What a mess,* I thought as I
followed everybody inside the house.

Seven

That afternoon John and Debbie took the four of us for a hike on the grounds. When we reached the top of a hill, we stopped and checked out the view.

"Awesome," Allison muttered as she threw herself down under a tree. "Can we rest now?"

As usual, I backed her up. "Yeah," I said, taking off my left shoe. "I think I still have a pebble in here from the Grand Canyon! Is that smuggling?"

"Yes, I could definitely get used to living here," Rosina declared, hands on hips, as she surveyed the estate.

Susette started to giggle. "You look like you'd like to plant the flag of Rosina and claim all you see as your own."

"Rosinaville . . . I like it!" Rosina grinned and sat down next to us.

"Girls, we need to talk," John began.

"Uh-oh." I leaned over and whispered to Allison, "I don't like the sound of this."

"Personally, I think talking is highly over-rated," Allison offered.

"Then maybe you two could just listen," Debbie said snidely.

"Look," John said, interrupting the beginning of a beautiful fight. "I think we should head back to London tonight."

"*No!*" the Adventurers shouted in unison.

"Please," Susette added. She's usually the only one who remembers her manners.

"I knew they wouldn't want to leave," John said, turning to Debbie.

"Come on, you guys." Debbie sat down next to us. "The Hastingses are having some family problems. The last thing they need is to have spectators."

"Uncle Randolph isn't family," I said.

"*Uncle* Randolph isn't family. That's a confused statement, even for you," Debbie joked.

"Well, Charles says he's evil," I muttered. To tell the truth, I was still pretty confused about the whole situation. It'd take more proof either way before I could make up my mind.

"I hardly think Charles is impartial," John said. "Charles is still having a tough time getting over his father's death. He'll come around."

"Losing your father isn't like losing a key or your wallet!" I shouted as I jumped to my feet. "How can you be so callous!"

"Hey." Debbie put out her hand and grabbed mine. "I know it's not." Debbie and I stared at each other for what seemed like a really long time. Then, she turned to John. "Why don't we just spend the night. We can leave right after breakfast."

John's eyebrows raised in surprise. "Okay," he said doubtfully. "But let's try and keep things on an even keel until then. Deal?" He looked at the four of us.

"Deal!" Allison jumped to her feet, and she and I took off running down the hill, Rosina and Susette following close behind.

Dinner wasn't served until late, but, as usual, I was hungry early. I had already bathed, and I was bored waiting around for the others to primp and preen. Allison says I'm so quick in the shower because there's so much less of me to wash. Rosina says it's just that I'm a piggy. The truth, as usual, probably lies somewhere in between. Actually, it *was* kind of my fault that the other girls were running late. They had decided that the project for the day was going to be the "beautification of Toni," so that there would be some sort of silly fairy-tale ending to this trip. You know, the typical handsome prince—or lord, in this case—sweeps the damsel in distress—or damsel *causing* distress, in this case—off her feet. I must admit, it all sounded pretty silly to me, but I kind of had no choice. You know how it is when your friends really want you to do something . . .

First, my hair. "But I like my curls," I whined as Rosina relentlessly pulled them straight with a big round brush.

"How can a round brush make straight hair," I complained as she tugged. "It doesn't make sense!"

"Neither does a lord falling for *you,* but that's the way it is," she muttered, giving a recalcitrant lock a fierce pull.

"Ouch!" I didn't mean to be a baby, but it hurt!

"Beauty is pain," she said.

"No, *you* are. Now let go!" I jumped up, the brush still stuck in my hair.

Allison shoved me back down. "Sit there and let her finish," Allison insisted. "You don't want to go around with half your head straight and half curly, now do you?"

"Fine," I muttered. "But I think you're nuts. All of you."

"Hey, why are you picking on me? I'm just sitting here, minding my own business!" Susette threw her hands up. "Jeez!"

"Done!" Rosina said, turning me around so that she could admire her handiwork. "I don't know why I'm surprised," she teased. "But your hair has a mind of its own."

"Makeup!" Allison said.

"But I always end up with it in all the wrong places," I protested. "Mascara on my cheeks, lipstick on my teeth. Can't I just use a little lip gloss and let it go at that?" I begged.

"No!" They all shouted in unison.

What can I say? I was outvoted.

I have to admit that by the time they were done with me, I looked pretty good. Shiny hair, rosy cheeks, thick lashes, and pouty lips. Like me, only more so. And kind of grown up.

Rosina lent me her black-velvet leggings, and Susette let me wear her new white blouse with ruffles on the sleeves that *she* hadn't even worn yet.

Nobody's shoes would fit me, but I had a pair of black espadrilles that looked pretty cool, so I was set.

Anyhow, as I was saying, there I was, dressed to kill, and no one even to get cranky with because the other three were getting ready now. So I headed down to the kitchen. Boredom always makes me hungry.

I got to the door of the kitchen and stopped dead. Uncle Randolph was stirring something in a huge black pot on the stove.

Now I'm no chef or anything, but I thought whatever it was smelled *awful*.

"They should like that!" he muttered as he stirred. "Better put something in to cover the smell though, or they'll never eat it." Randolph reached into a cabinet and pulled out a jar with a label I didn't recognize. Then he added three tablespoons of an almond-colored liquid to the pot.

"The little buggers will never know what hit them!" he said. He smiled. "They'll be dead before morning!"

Uncle Randolph left the pot and walked out into the garden. I was too stunned to move. *Never know what hit them . . . I* thought. *Dead before morning. He is trying to kill Charles and Sarah. Charles is right!* My thoughts were whirring around in my head so fast, my body didn't have any energy left to move!

Now, I know that in the past I have been accused of jumping to conclusions. Leaping before looking. Putting the cart before the horse and going off half cocked. But this was different. I had *heard* Uncle Randolph say he was trying to kill "them." How could there be any question about his meaning?

I wasn't sure what to do. After all, I'd never been in this kind of situation before. One thing I *did* know was that no one should be eating that soup! I was about to slip into the kitchen and pour it down the sink when Uncle Randolph came back into the kitchen. This time, John was with him.

"So, do you really think it will work?"

John asked. "I've always had a real problem with them."

"Sure," Randolph assured him. "Dead in a matter of hours."

"Good." John grinned. "Those little pests have really gotten on my nerves.

I couldn't believe what I was hearing. I mean, I knew we'd caused some trouble along the way, but I'd had *no* idea John was *that* mad at us. Mad enough to want to *kill* us!

I backed quietly out of the kitchen alcove and ran upstairs to tell the others. I took the stairs two at a time and nearly collided with Sarah on the landing.

"Sorry!" I said as I tried to scoot around her.

"Wait, please!" she answered, grabbing my hand.

Don't get me wrong, I like kids, but the last thing I wanted to do at that moment was talk to Sarah. Not when all our lives were at stake!

"I gotta go . . . I gotta find Charles," I said, trying to release her grip.

"He's on a walk with Mum," she replied, not letting go of my hand. Who would have thought she was so strong?

"Then Debbie. I need Debbie." I was

still trying to break away from her by taking small steps backward.

"She's in the back garden with John." She smiled at me. "We could play."

Suddenly, I felt very sorry for Sarah. She had lost her father; her mother had a new boyfriend; her brother was too busy dealing with his grief to really spend time with her, and when he did, he tended to treat her like a baby. But, sorry for her or not, I had to warn everyone about Uncle Randolph's impending culinary attack.

"Later, Sarah, I promise!" I broke free, tried to ignore the pained look on Sarah's face, and dashed down the hallway to our room.

"You're never going to believe it!" I blurted as I slammed the door behind me.

Three heads in various stages of makeup readiness turned to look at me.

"Believe what?" Susette asked as she jumped to her feet.

"What's going on?" Allison said at the same time.

"Charles was right!" I began to pace. I was so excited, I just couldn't stand still. "Uncle Randolph is trying to kill him. And Sarah."

"Don't bump me, I'm putting on mascara!" Rosina warned as I headed toward her.

"You're nuts," Allison said, shaking her head.

"No, I mean it. And John is in on it, too. He wants to kill *us!*" I sat down hard on the bed.

"Now you've *really* lost it," Allison said. "Something must have shaken loose when you were hanging over the edge of the balloon today."

"Really," I insisted. "Listen to this . . ."

I told them about what I had seen and heard.

"Are you sure?" Susette looked skeptical. "I can't believe you heard right."

"I'm sure you didn't." Rosina had finished her mascara. "Who would want to kill *me?*" she asked.

The three of us looked at each other, but no one said the obvious.

"I'm *positive*. Come see for yourselves."

We trooped down the hall commando style, and climbed quietly down the stairs.

"Come on," I whispered as we turned the corner to the kitchen. I peeked around the half-open door and saw John and Randolph stirring the pot.

"See," I hissed.

Allison poked her head around next. "So?" she whispered. "They're cooking. What's the big deal?"

"Ready!" Randolph announced proudly. I grabbed Allison's arm.

"They really won't notice the taste?" John asked.

"Nope. And they'll be dead by morning," Randolph added.

Well, I'd had all I could take. "How dare you!" I shouted as I jumped out from behind the door.

"Toni!" John looked startled. "How dare I what?" he asked.

"Don't play Mr. Innocent with me!" I warned. "We all heard you." I flung open the door the rest of the way so he could see the other girls.

"Heard what?" Randolph asked.

"About your poisoning us. 'Won't notice the taste, dead by morning,' " I quoted.

They still looked confused.

"That!" I pointed at the pot on the stove.

Suddenly Randolph started to laugh. Then John joined him.

"What?" I cried. I *hate* being laughed at.

Besides, I didn't think two grown men plotting to murder a bunch of innocent children was very funny.

Just then Debbie came in from the garden. "Lucy wants to know if it's ready," she asked. "Hey. What's so funny?"

"They thought . . ." John began before bursting out laughing again.

"Toni accused . . ." Randolph started to explain before he dissolved into giggles.

"You two are hopeless," Debbie said, hands on hips. "I'll take the bug poison out to Lucy myself." She grabbed the pot off the stove and stomped out the door.

"Bug poison?" I whispered.

Behind me I could hear Allison, Rosina and Susette trying not to crack up. They failed. Snorts of laughter exploded out of them.

I felt pretty stupid, but I figured it was better to laugh with them then stand there being laughed at.

I'll never hear the end of this, I thought as I tried to get an apology out in between my giggles. *Ever!* (And so far, I've been right.)

* * *

We had calmed down by dinner that evening. Sarah was still shaken from her near accident (and now I felt *really* bad that I hadn't stopped to play with her); Charles was still angry at both his Uncle Randolph and his mother; Uncle Randolph was still angry at Charles (as was Lady Hastings); the rest of us were embarrassed at having been witness to such family discord; and I was still humiliated for mistaking bug poison for killer soup. The only up side was that John and Randolph had agreed not to tell Lucy, Debbie, and Charles about what a fool I'd been. I was really beginning to believe that Randolph was an okay guy and that Charles was all wrong in his assumptions about his uncle.

No one argued when John suggested an early bedtime so that we could get a jump on the morning. Especially me. Saving a life and making a major fool of myself in the space of a few short hours had really taken its toll!

Something woke me. I mean, one minute I was asleep, and then I wasn't. I opened my eyes. The room was dark except for the shaft of moonlight coming in through the lace curtains.

"Allison," I whispered.

Nothing. No response.

I got out of bed, shoved my feet into my slippers, and padded over to her bed. "Hey," I said, shaking her shoulder, "get up." Then I ducked. As I mentioned, we've been best friends for almost all our lives. I knew what kind of person she was when woken in the middle of the night. A mean one.

"What?" she said as her fist flew. I guess it's hard having four older brothers.

"It's me, Toni. Stop swinging, slugger."

Allison sat up in bed and rubbed her eyes. "What? Is it morning?"

"No. Did you hear something?" I asked.

"Yes. You telling me to get up," she answered, looking grumpy.

"No. I heard a noise."

Just then, Susette and Rosina came into our room.

"You heard it, too?" Rosina asked.

"Yeah," I said. "I did, but Sleeping Beauty here snored right through it," I added, messing Allison's hair.

"I don't snore!" She pouted. "And leave my hair alone."

"What was it?" Susette asked.

"Sounded like something falling," Rosina guessed.

"Come on." I pulled on my bathrobe over my T-shirt. "Let's go see what is was."

The hallway was pitch black. Well, except for the moonlight coming through a window at one end of the hall. It took a while for our eyes to adjust so that we could see anything at all.

"It came from above us," I said, pointing at the staircase at the other end of the hall. "I bet what we heard was something hitting the ceiling above our rooms."

Single file we made our way down the hall to the staircase. When we reached the top, we weren't sure which way to go.

"This is scary," Rosina whispered. "Do you think it's a burglar?"

"Or a ghost?" Susette asked. "Not that I believe in them, or anything," she added quickly.

"Gee, that was helpful," I whispered angrily. "As if we weren't scared enough walking around in a four-hundred-year old house in the dead of night. We feel *much* better, now."

"We *do* have a weapon," Allison said, brandishing a can of hairspray she'd kept concealed in a pocket of her bathrobe.

I stifled a snort of laughter. "What? You're going to do a makeover on a ghost? Or better yet, beautify a burglar?"

"Fine." Allison was offended. "It hurts when this stuff gets in your eyes, you know. And what are *you* going to do, scare the ghosts with your sleep face?"

I stuck out my tongue at her, but it was too dark for her to see it. *I guess that won't work on a ghost or burglar either,* I thought nervously.

Huddled in a group, we shuffled down the hall. Then we heard it. Footsteps. Only this time, they were behind us. *Right* behind us.

Only one thing to do. I wheeled around and grabbed the burglar around the knees. "Gotcha!" I mumbled, as I knocked him to the floor. The other Adventurers piled on top of us.

"Let me up, you silly twit," came the angry whisper.

We froze. "Charles?" I asked.

"No, the King of Spain!" Charles answered.

We untangled ourselves as quietly and as quickly as we could. "Sorry," I muttered. "We heard a noise."

"Me, too," he said. We realized we were still sitting on the floor and scrambled to our feet. Someone was stepping on my bathrobe, so it took me two tries. Typical.

"Remember I told you valuable family heirlooms were turning up missing?" Charles said in a whisper.

"How can something turn up missing?" Rosina asked.

"Shut up!" we all hissed.

"I think whoever is stealing from the family is upstairs right now. And I bet I know who it is. Come on," Charles urged. "Follow me."

Once again, single file, this time with Charles as the leader, we made our way down the hall. There was definitely someone in the room at the end. By the time we reached the door, I could hear someone moving and I was beginning to doubt the wisdom of creeping around an old house trying to catch a bad guy in the middle of the night, wearing nothing but our nightshirts and bathrobes, with only a can of hairspray as protection.

"Follow me!" Charles shouted, slamming open the door. "Gotcha!" He tackled Uncle Randolph, who dropped the vase he was putting into an open suitcase. Luckily, the vase, which I later found out was very old and *very* expensive, fell unharmed on an Oriental carpet that was half rolled up by Randolph's feet.

"I knew it was you!" Charles shouted as he struggled with his uncle.

Now, Randolph had six inches and maybe fifty pounds on Charles, but Charles had real anger and, of course, the Adventurers to back him up.

"Come on!" I urged, as I grabbed one of Uncle Randolph's arms and sat on it.

Within moments he was pinned, each of us on a limb, and Charles on his stomach. Charles drew back his arm as if he was going to punch his uncle, and I must confess, at that point I closed my eyes.

"What on earth is going on here!" My eyes popped open. Lady Hastings burst into the room and grabbed Charles's fist just in time.

"This is who has been stealing from us, Mum. I told you he was stealing. I told you . . ."

"Charles, get up this instant."

"But . . ."

"Charles. Your uncle hasn't been stealing." She finally looked at us. "Get up."

Well, Charles might ignore his mother—I mean, I sometimes ignore mine—but *I* wasn't about to ignore *his*. I got up, as did the others.

"Listen to me, Charles. Your uncle has been helping me make ends meet by selling pieces of art. Get up this instant!"

Charles, who was still perched on Randolph's chest, looked between his uncle and his mother.

"I'm not getting up until I get some straight answers. Why sell these treasures? They've been in our family forever," he argued, his voice a bit wobbly.

"Because your mother needs the money, Charles," Randolph answered, looking squashed, but distinctly relieved that he wasn't going to get hit.

"Fine. If money is the problem, I'll get a job," Charles said. He looked at his mother. "Why didn't you tell me our financial situation was this bad? You should have told me the truth." He shook his head in disgust and looked now at Randolph. "Isn't it bad enough that you killed your own brother? Now, you're trying to ruin this family by selling off our heritage!"

Even to me, Charles wasn't making a lot of sense, but grief has a way of making people a little nutty.

"Charles!" Lady Hastings pulled Charles off Randolph and slapped him a good one across the face. "Your father killed himself. He knew the winds were too high that day for ballooning, but he wanted to go up anyway. I tried to stop him, but he wouldn't listen. You know how stubborn your father could be."

"Then *you* could have stopped him." Charles glared at his uncle, who had risen to his feet.

Then Randolph did something totally unexpected. He started to cry. "I tried, Charlie. I tried. But I couldn't persuade him not to go up. I wish I had been able to convince him. I wish he hadn't died." Randolph stopped and took a deep breath. "He was my brother, Charlie. And I miss him too."

Suddenly, Charles began to cry, and before I knew what was happening, Charles was hugging Randolph. Then Lady Hastings started to cry, and then, I did, too. Soon, we were *all* crying and hugging. It got really mushy for a few minutes there.

When we'd all dried out a bit, and Lady Hastings had passed out tissues (why is it, by the way, that adults always have Kleenex handy?), Charles spoke up.

"Look, Randolph, I'm sorry I jumped you," he said, sticking out his hand.

"Apology accepted." Randolph offered his own hand. "Charles," he said, dropping his hand and putting an arm around Lady Hastings, "I want to ask you a question."

The Adventurers had drawn away from the family group and were trying to be invisible against the wall. But our ears were working overtime!

Randolph drew a deep breath. "I love your mother and want to marry her. I have enough money, enough so that the house can be yours again, not open to the public five days a week. And I intend to recover as many of the Hastings's heirlooms your mother has had to sell as I can. But your mother won't say yes to my proposal of marriage unless you approve."

There was a moment of silence. I could see Charles fighting with old memories, old beliefs, and new facts. I thought about how hard it would be for me if my mother wanted to remarry. I was holding my breath.

Lady Hastings looked like she was holding her breath as well.

"I'm not your father and never will be," Randolph added. "But I would like to be your uncle again, and not your enemy."

"Okay," Charles whispered. "Okay."

Suddenly, everyone was crying again. England is a *very* wet country.

Eight

At breakfast the next morning, I filled John in on the night's excitement.

"You did *what* in the middle of the night?" John put his head in his hands. "I do not believe you guys."

"But it all turned out okay," I insisted. "Now Lady Hastings is going to marry Randolph, Charles doesn't hate him anymore, and . . ."

"And you are all invited to the wedding." Lady Hastings came into the room, with Sarah at her side.

"I'm going to be a flower girl," Sarah announced.

Susette grinned at her. "You'll be wonderful."

"I'm really sorry," John said. "I mean . . ."

"There is nothing to be sorry for. You've all been wonderful. I owe a lot to

Toni," she said as she reached out to pat Sarah's head. "She's a very brave girl."

Rosina's mouth was hanging open. "A royal wedding. Do we really get to go?"

"I certainly hope so," Lady Hastings said. "I'd like you four to be in it."

Charles joined us at the breakfast table. "You will come back for it, won't you?" He smiled at me across his tea.

I nodded. My mouth was too full of crumpet to talk.

"That's very kind of you," Debbie said, casting a significant look at John. "I just love weddings."

Suddenly, I had this overwhelming desire for some fresh air. I quickly swallowed what I was chewing.

"Want to take a walk?" I asked, looking at Charles.

"Sure," Rosina said jumping up.

I glared at her.

"But not right now," she added lamely, sitting down again.

Charles and I wandered out in to the back gardens. As we walked up the hill away from the house, he took my hand. I prayed it wasn't all sweaty. Or greasy with buttery crumpet!

We walked in silence for a while, not stopping until we reached a large tree near the top of the hill. He held my hand the whole way.

"I really do want you to come back," he said, turning me to face him. "Will you be my date for the wedding?"

I felt myself go all hot and cold at the same time. I hadn't ever had an official date. And my first one was going to be with a lord! And a really nice guy, too. "Sure." I smiled at him. "You okay about this wedding stuff?"

He shrugged. "I wish my father hadn't died. And I really do wish my mother wouldn't ever remarry, but that's not fair to her. Sarah needs a father, Mum needs a husband. Randolph's okay. You know, I liked him a lot *before* my father's death. I guess I kind of forgot that for a while." He looked down for a moment. I knew he was thinking about his father. He looked back at me and smiled. "But if there has to be a wedding, I'm glad you'll be there."

I looked up at him and smiled, and then it happened. Just like in the movies. He leaned down, and placed his mouth on mine. I felt his lips part slightly, and we kissed. I mean the weak-in-the-knees, but-terflies-in-the-stomach, bubbles-in-your-brain kind of kiss.

It was wonderful, so we did it again.

Nine

It was raining again as we left for Heathrow Airport. Randolph had insisted on sending us off in style. A huge limo had picked us up at Mrs. Beasley's that afternoon.

"Now do you feel better about missing the Crown Jewels, Rosina?" Debbie asked as we slipped into its plush velveteen interior.

"Much!" she answered as she wriggled into her seat.

"And don't even *think* about getting us bumped up again!" I warned. "I don't want to spend another flight trapped in a bathroom."

"Okay, I won't. Anyway, I'm thinking about our *next* trip. Spain. It's going to be fabulous." Rosina babbled about her family for the entire forty-five-minute drive to the airport.

"I hope you have better luck with your

family than I had with mine at first," Allison said with a laugh. We had visited Allison's cousin in New York, and it had been really tough going for a while. The girls hadn't seen each other since they were little, and they'd both changed so much, it looked as if they'd never be friends again. "Although Letitia and I did get things worked out before I left," Allison added.

"I don't care about going on to Spain," I said. "I wish we could stay here." I felt really sad at the thought that I wouldn't see Charles until the wedding. Whenever that would be.

Susette and Allison made kissing noises. "Gee," Rosina said sarcastically, "I wonder why."

John and Debbie got the bags checked and got us seated on the plane with a minimum of fuss.

"Now look!" John said as the plane took off. "I want to make one thing perfectly clear. I want *no* trouble in Spain. No danger, as in hanging out of hot air balloons, no sneaking around in the middle of the night, no mysteries, no nothing. Promise?"

We did, but I knew that it was hopeless. When the Adventurers were traveling together . . . excitement was sure to be on the itinerary!

Hi!

I lived in England the summer I was twenty. I had the best time! Even though I was already living away from home at college in New York City, for some reason, living in England I felt really, *really* far away from home. Anyway, I was pretty lonely until I met Gordon. He's the guy I dedicated this book to. We've been the closest friends for twelve years now.

Gordon was running the stable right in the heart of London and I ended up teaching there. We spent the long summer days working with horses and the long summer nights hanging out in Covent Garden, having fun.

I never did get to see a country estate, and all the hot air balloon rides I have taken have been in order to make a skydive, but England *is* truly one of my favorite places to visit. Give it a try!

See you in Spain!
Love,

Nally

P.S. Where have you been? Where do you want to go? Write and tell me and I'll try to send the Adventurers there!

The four friends and their chaperones, John and Debbie, are visting Rosina's family on the coast of Spain. Everyone is excited about staying in an old castle . . . especially when they hear it's *haunted.* Susette doesn't believe in ghosts, but when she explores the attic—and stumbles upon a portrait of a girl who looks *exactly* like Rosina—she starts to wonder . . .

After an old diary reveals that the mysterious girl is Rosina's distant relative, Rosina suddenly begins acting strangely. Then Susette learns that the girl was murdered on her birthday, which happens to be *Rosina's* birthday, too . . . and it's only two days away! Susette *knows* there has to be a logical explanation for all the weird things that are happening—and she's determined to save Rosina from whatever supernatural forces—or "real" spooks—are out to get her friend!